D1395582

THE AMAZING ADVENTURES OF
Ulysses

Retold by
Vivian Webb
and Heather Amery

Adapted by Katie Daynes

Illustrated by
Stephen Cartwright

Reading Consultant: Alison Kelly
Roehampton University

Contents

Some pages show you how to say Greek names.
The parts of the words in **bold** should be stressed.

Chapter 1

A wooden horse

Long ago, a Trojan prince stole Helen, a Greek princess. He took her to his city, Troy. At once, a Greek king, named Ulysses*, set sail with many other Greek kings and their armies to rescue her.

3

* say **you**-lis-sees

Ulysses and the soldiers came face to face with the Trojans outside the city. The Greek men fought bravely.

But the Trojan army wasn't their only problem. The city of Troy was protected by huge walls.

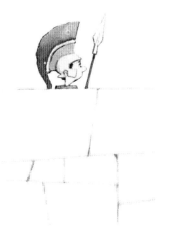

The Greek armies fought the Trojans for ten years, but they couldn't get into Troy.

After hundreds of battles and thousands of injuries, they still hadn't rescued Helen.

But Ulysses was not going to give up. He thought of a cunning trick.

The next day, the Trojans awoke to a surprise. Outside the city walls, the Greek camp had disappeared. In its place stood a giant wooden horse.

Every single one of the Greek ships had vanished too.

"We've won, we've won!" shouted the people of Troy.

They wheeled the wooden horse through the gates into the city and partied until midnight.

Unknown to the Trojans, Ulysses and his men were hiding inside the horse.

While everyone was sleeping, they climbed down a rope ladder. Then they crept to the city gates and opened them.

Outside, the rest of the Greek army was waiting.

The soldiers had sailed back to Troy in the dark of night.

When morning came, the city of Troy woke up to a nightmare.

The Trojan men tried to fight but the Greek soldiers killed them all.

Then the Greeks stole all of their treasure, set fire to buildings and rescued Helen. The war with Troy – the Trojan War – was over.

But for Ulysses and his men, the adventures had just begun...

Chapter 2

The Cyclops

The Greek kings shared out the treasure between them. Then all the ships set sail for home. But Ulysses and his men got lost.

12

After two weeks at sea, they landed on an island to look for more food and water. All they had left to drink was some wine, which they took with them.

At the top of a cliff, they found a cave. It was full of huge cheeses and vast buckets of milk. The men called out but there was no answer.

"Let's go in and eat now," suggested Ulysses. "Then we can wait for the owner."

As they ate, a shadow fell on the men. They looked up and saw a one-eyed giant – a Cyclops.

He drove his sheep into the cave and rolled a rock across the entrance, blocking them in...

15

His one enormous eye glared at the Greeks.

"Who are you?" he roared.

As Ulysses tried to explain, the Cyclops snatched up two men.

He crushed them in his fists and ate them both.

Then the Cyclops gave a loud burp, lay down and went to sleep. The men begged Ulysses to kill him before he ate them too.

You could stab him now.

"No," said their wise king. "If I kill him, who's going to move that heavy rock and set us free?"

The next morning, the Cyclops went out of the cave. He moved the heavy rock back into place, trapping the men inside.

Ulysses and his men had to think fast.

When the Cyclops returned,
Ulysses offered him some wine.

"What is your name?" asked the
Cyclops.

"Nobody," replied Ulysses,
pouring out more wine.

"What a funny name," laughed
the Cyclops and fell asleep.

Ulysses picked up a pole that he had sharpened and hidden. He heated the end in the fire.

The men tiptoed toward the giant. They plunged the red-hot pole into his eye.

The Cyclops roared out in pain. Everyone on the island rushed to see what was wrong.

"Nobody has hurt me," cried the Cyclops. "Nobody poked my eye out and I can't see!"

"If nobody has hurt you, then stop crying like a baby," said the other giants, walking away.

The blind and furious Cyclops rolled away the rock. He waited for the Greeks to come out. But Ulysses had already planned their escape.

I'm going to get you Mr. Nobody.

Each man was tied onto the belly of a sheep. All the Cyclops could feel was wool and horns.

Too late, the giant realized he'd been tricked. Ulysses and his men had already escaped.

Chapter 3

Circe and her spells

The Greeks sailed away laughing.
But they had made a new enemy –
the Cyclops' father, Poseidon*.

24

* say poss-**eye**-don

Poseidon was god of the sea.
He hated Ulysses and his crew
for hurting one of his sons.

"They won't be laughing for very
long," he snarled.

Soon, Ulysses' ship had landed on another island. Ulysses divided his men into two groups.

One man, Eurylochus*, would lead half the crew in search of food and water. Ulysses would stay with the rest of the men to guard his ship.

26

* say you-**ril**-o-kus

Eurylochus and his men walked for hours. They couldn't find anything to eat or drink and they didn't meet a soul.

Finally, one of the men saw a wisp of smoke rising above the trees.

The smoke led them to a palace and a beautiful woman.

The woman led them into a grand hall. A feast was laid out on the table.

"You are my guests," said the woman. "Please, eat!"

Cheers!

Between mouthfuls, one man asked her name.

"I am Circe*," she said, and filled the men's cups with wine.

28

* say **sir**-see

The Greeks ate, drank and sang a lot. They didn't notice that Eurylochus wasn't there.

He didn't trust Circe so he was spying from outside. What happened next made him gasp in horror.

One wave of Circe's magic wand turned the men into pigs!

Eurylochus raced back to the ship. He told the others what he had seen.

Without delay, Ulysses set off to rescue his friends.

On the way, Hermes*, who was the messenger for the gods, flew up to him.

"The goddess Athene* sends you this magic flower," he told Ulysses. "Eat it and you will be safe from Circe's tricks."

* say **her**-meez and a-**thee**-nee

At the palace, Circe invited Ulysses inside for some wine. Behind his back, she poured some poison into his cup.

This will fix him...

Ulysses drank the wine. He wasn't afraid of Circe's magic.

Then she tapped him with her wand. He jumped up.

"Your evil magic can't harm me," he cried. "Now take me to my crew."

Help! My magic hasn't worked.

Circe was scared. She led him to the pig sty right away.

Circe smeared a potion onto the pigs' snouts. Magically, they changed back into men.

Whew! I'm me again.

The men were frightened of Circe but she promised not to work any more magic on them. If she did, she knew Ulysses would kill her.

She prepared a great feast that lasted a year. The men from the ship came to join in too.

When the men decided to go, Circe was very sad. She had fallen in love with Ulysses. But she gave them food and warned them of dangers that lay ahead.

Chapter 4

The bewitching Sirens

The Greeks' next challenge was to sail past the Sirens' island. This was trickier than it sounds.

Sirens were sea nymphs who bewitched passing sailors with their beautiful songs. Men would sail closer and closer to the island, until they wrecked their ships on the rocks and drowned.

Follow that song!

Circe had warned Ulysses about the Sirens. He knew just what to do.

Ulysses cut up pieces of beeswax and gave them to his men to use as earplugs.

This is great! I can't even hear the gulls.

But Ulysses wanted to hear what was so special about the Sirens' singing. He told his men to tie him tightly to the mast.

When the Sirens began to sing their delicious songs, only Ulysses was bewitched.

"Untie me from the ropes!" he pleaded. His crew just rowed on. They couldn't hear a thing.

How rude!

The Sirens were astonished to see the Greek ship sail straight past their island.

Chapter 5

The whirlpool monster

When they thought they were safe, the crew unplugged their ears and untied their leader.

Suddenly there was a sound of angry water whooshing around. They were about to be sucked into a whirlpool.

"Pull harder, men," yelled Ulysses. "Keep near the cliff."

The men were so busy avoiding the whirlpool that they didn't notice a six-headed monster reach down from a cave in the cliff.

The monster was called Scylla* and she was very hungry.

* say **sill**-a

Each of her six necks stretched across the sea and each mouth picked up a man.

The men begged for help but she swallowed them whole.

Chapter 6

The sea god's revenge

The terrified Greeks rowed away
from Scylla as fast as they could.
But a raging storm blew up and
snapped the mast in two. Poseidon
was getting his revenge.

Then a giant wave flooded the ship and all the men drowned, except Ulysses. He clung to the broken mast and somehow reached the shore.

Next morning, a princess found him collapsed on the sand. She took him to see her father, the king.

Ulysses told the king about his adventures.

"I will help you," promised the king. "One of my ships will take you home this evening."

Don't worry. Your island isn't far away.

Ulysses fell asleep on the king's ship. When they reached his island, the sailors carried him to the beach.

At that moment, Poseidon surfed by in his chariot.

"Ulysses should have died in that storm," he grumbled. "I will punish those who helped him."

And he turned the king's ship and its sailors into stone.

Chapter 7

Home at last

For the first time in twenty years, Ulysses woke up on his home island. A lady nearby was watching him. "The goddess Athene!" whispered Ulysses.

48

"You can't go home yet," she said. "You've been away so long everyone thinks you're dead."

Things have changed.

"Many men are at the palace now. They want to marry your wife, Penelope, and kill your son Telemachus*."

49

Athene had a plan. She gave
Ulysses a disguise and sent him to
the pig keeper's hut.

The pig keeper thought Ulysses
was a hungry beggar. He invited
him in for some food and a chat.

Then Athene sent Ulysses' son, Prince Telemachus, to the same hut. When the pig keeper was out of the room, Athene used her magic to remove Ulysses' disguise.

Telemachus was no longer looking at a beggar. He was looking at his father.

Quickly, Ulysses and his son
talked about how to save
Penelope and the kingdom.

The next day, Ulysses went to
the palace with the pig keeper.
Once again, he was in disguise.

If you want
King Ulysses' palace,
it's over there.

Ulysses pretended to beg inside the great hall. Dozens of men were feasting and boasting about who would marry Queen Penelope.

They only gave Ulysses a few crumbs to eat.

"Go away, you smelly beggar," they said.

When Queen Penelope heard there was a beggar in the palace, she asked her nurse to fetch him.

"Maybe he has news of Ulysses!" she said to herself.

"Don't be sad," said Ulysses. "Your husband is very close by."

He hid his face so that Penelope wouldn't recognize him.

Suddenly, the goddess Athene put an idea into Penelope's head.

I know! Tomorrow, I'll give those men an impossible challenge.

That night, Ulysses slept on the floor of the great hall.

In the morning, the men arrived as usual. They were surprised when they saw Queen Penelope carrying Ulysses' bow.

"Gentlemen," she announced, "I will marry the man who can use this bow. All he needs to do is shoot an arrow through these twelve axes."

They're very heavy.

She gave the bow to a servant and left the hall.

All the men wanted to show their strength and win the queen.

They tried and they tried but none of them could even put the string on the bow.

When the men gave up, Ulysses stepped forward.

May I try?

At first the men laughed, but Ulysses didn't listen.
He picked up the bow, put on the string and fired an arrow straight through the axes.

The men gasped as Athene changed back Ulysses' rags into his clothes.

I am King Ulysses and I have come to reclaim my kingdom!

Ulysses and Telemachus fought all the men who wanted to steal the kingdom.

The men tried to escape but the doors were locked. Soon, Ulysses and his son had killed them all.

When Penelope heard what had happened, she rushed into the hall. Could this man really be Ulysses? Maybe the gods were tricking her.

It's me, darling.

How can I be sure?

Penelope thought of one last test. She asked the nurse to move the bed out of her room, so this stranger could rest on it.

"But that's impossible," said Ulysses. "I built that bedroom around a tall olive tree. The bed is part of the tree!"

"Oh Ulysses, it really is you," said Penelope, smiling.

After years of travel and trouble, the family was together at last.

Ulysses was written about 3,000 years ago by a Greek poet named Homer. In his story, called *The Odyssey,* Ulysses was known as Odysseus. Here, he has been given his Roman name of Ulysses.

Series Editor: Lesley Sims
Designed by Katarina Dragoslavić

With thanks to Luke Taylor

This edition first published in 2007 by Usborne Publishing Ltd., Usborne House, 83-85 Saffron Hill, London EC1N 8RT, England.
www.usborne.com
Copyright © 2007, 2003, 1982 Usborne Publishing Ltd.